Soap Box Racing

By Edward Radlauer

AN ELK GROVE BOOK

 CHILDRENS PRESS, CHICAGO

Library of Congress Cataloging in Publication Data

Radlauer, Edward.
  Soap box racing.

  (Ready, get set, go series)
  SUMMARY: Photographs and brief text present the
steps involved in building a soap box racer and
entering a soap box derby.

  "An Elk Grove book."

  1. Soap box derbies. [1. Soap box derbies]

I. Title.
GV1029.7.R27   796.6   73-6658
ISBN 0-516-07423-7

15 16 17 18 19 20 21 22 23 24 25 R 87 86 85 84 83 82

Ready, Get Set, Go Books

Ready

Motorcycle Mania

Get Set

Fast, Faster, Fastest

Go

Soap Box Racing

How would you like
to have a Soap Box Derby racer?
You can't buy one.
No one can buy a Soap Box racer.

If you can't buy a Soap Box racer,
how do you get one?
You build it.
You build it yourself.

You can buy wood, nails, and glue
for building your racer.
But you do all the work.
No one can help.

Even if you had a lot of money,
you couldn't spend much on your racer.
All you can spend is $35.00.

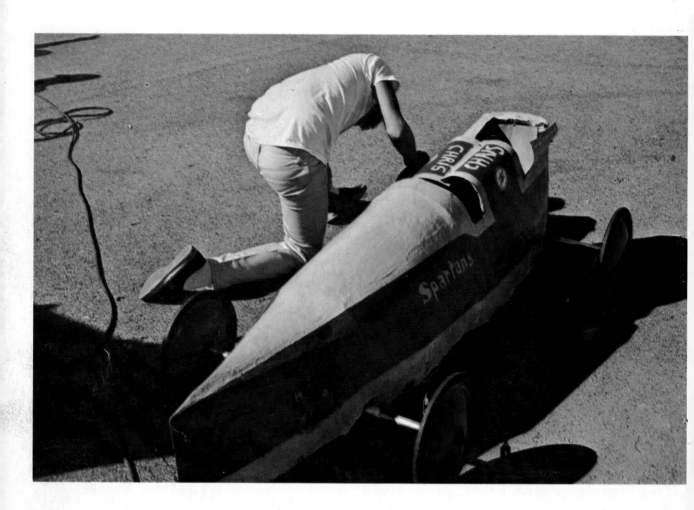

To build a racer you need plans.
The plans are in a Soap Box Derby rule book.
The Chevrolet Company
makes the rule book.
You can get it from a company
that sells Chevrolet cars.

The plans tell you how much wood,
nails, and glue you need.
The plans also tell
how big your racer should be.

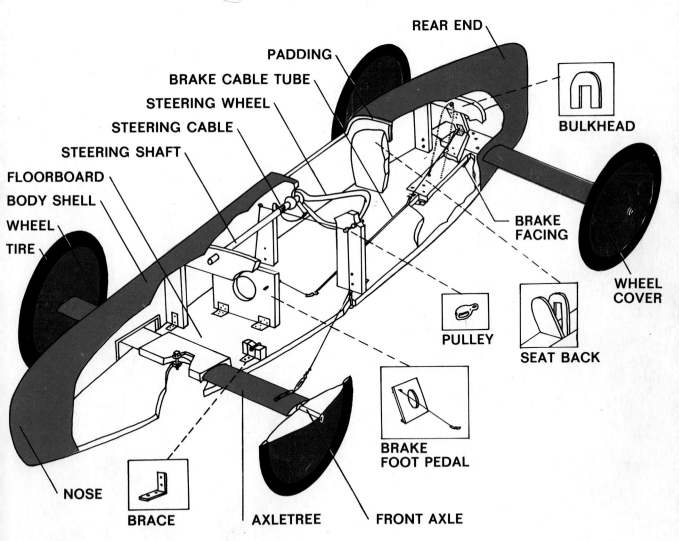

REAR END

PADDING

BRAKE CABLE TUBE

STEERING WHEEL

STEERING CABLE

STEERING SHAFT

FLOORBOARD

BODY SHELL

WHEEL

TIRE

BULKHEAD

BRAKE FACING

WHEEL COVER

PULLEY

SEAT BACK

NOSE

BRACE

AXLETREE

FRONT AXLE

BRAKE FOOT PEDAL

11

Before you start to build your racer,
find out how to do it.
Look at cars other people built.
Then build your own.

Your racer will need
a body, wheels, and a brake.
The brake works
by rubbing on the ground.

15

You can build the body
of your racer out of wood,
cardboard, or fiberglass.
You cannot build your racer
out of metal.

Inside the wood, cardboard,
or fiberglass body of your racer,
you will have a frame.
The frame holds your racer together.

While you are building your racer,
you can use practice wheels.
But on the day of the race
you take off the practice wheels
and put on the official Soap Box Derby wheels.

Before you can race,
you sign up with the Derby Officials.
After you tell the officials
how you built your car,
you get a Derby helmet.

Still, you cannot race
until the Derby Officials inspect your racer.
They inspect the body, frame, brake,
and wheels.

If your car passes inspection,
it's time to get weighed.
You and your car go on the scale together.
The rules say that a driver and his car
together must weigh 250 pounds or less.

While you wait to race,
you stay in the pits.
You are in the pits
with other racing people.
All other people wait outside the pits.

The Derby race is downhill.
The track is almost 1000 feet long.
On a 1000-foot downhill track
you can go fast.

During a Soap Box Derby race you may go 35 or 40 miles per hour. At that speed you have to know how to steer.

If you don't know how to steer,
your racer may go uphill,
not downhill. If you go uphill,
that's not so good.

Three cars race at once.
The winner of each three-car race
goes on to race other winners.

The finish line
is where your friends can watch.
All your friends watch and hope
you will be first across the finish line.

And the race is over!
You went fast, very fast,
and you drove a good race.
Did your friends see you win?

The end?